ON THE WAY TO KINDERGARTEN

Virginia Kroll

ILLUSTRATED BY

Elisabeth Schlossberg

G. P. PUTNAM'S SONS

When you were NEWBORN, you ate, burped, and cried,
And yawned with your cute gummy mouth opened wide.
You slept in your bassinet, stroller, or swing,
Calmed by the lullabies Grammy would sing.

When you were ONE, you pulled yourself up
And drank all your juice from your red sippy cup.
You messed lots of diapers and drooled down your shirt

And tried eating ants and a handful of dirt.

When you were TWO, you got your big bed
And picked panda sheets and a dinosaur spread.
You giggled and clapped when you saw the full moon.

You ate yogurt all by yourself with a spoon.

When you were THREE, you skipped down the hall,
Pedaled your tricycle, caught your first ball.

You liked the same storybooks day after day
And molded a snake out of modeling clay.

When you were FOUR, you tried figs and kiwis
And blew shiny bubbles that danced on the breeze.
You brushed your own teeth till they sparkled white-clean.

You drew trees and turtles and colored them green.

But NOW when we eat at that great bagel place,
You put back your own tray and wipe your own face.
You sit—no more booster seat—tall in the booth.

You're just about ready to lose your first tooth.

You can name all the beasts in your Noah's ark set
And help fill the fish tank without getting wet.
You don't need the stool now to reach the snack shelf.

You get on the swing and pump all by yourself!

You're teaching your best friend the ABC song.
You put back your building blocks where they belong.

You help carry groceries home in a bag.
Last Tuesday you said the whole Pledge to the flag.

You print your first name in *almost* a straight line
And count all the way from one to twenty-nine.
You zip up your jacket and dial the phone

And play tinkly tunes on your new xylophone.

You buckle your seat belt for trips in the car.
You've saved thirty coins in your "wish money" jar.

You know all the seasons and days of the week.
You find secret spots when you play hide-and-seek.

You've even made sandwiches and combed your hair.
You rode a gold carousel horse at the fair.
Last time you were sniffly, you blew your own nose.

With Hippo, you put on the best puppet shows.

You play superheroes in costumes and capes.

You know all your colors and most of your shapes.
In swim class, you paddled the length of the pool . . .

And suddenly, here you are, going to school!

Just think—the exciting adventures that wait!
Imagine the things that you'll craft and create.
You're cool, smart, and funny; you know things galore . . .

'Cause now you are FIVE
and a baby no more!!!!

With love to Zachary and Sabrina Combs,
wonderful kids who are babies no more—V. K.

To my daughter Anna, who won't be a baby anymore—E. S.

G. P. PUTNAM'S SONS
A division of Penguin Young Readers Group
Published by The Penguin Group
Penguin Group (USA) Inc., 375 Hudson Street, New York, NY 10014, U.S.A.
Penguin Group (Canada), 90 Eglinton Avenue East, Suite 700, Toronto, Ontario, Canada M4P 2Y3 (a division of Pearson Penguin Canada Inc.)
Penguin Books Ltd, 80 Strand, London WC2R 0RL, England.
Penguin Ireland, 25 St. Stephen's Green, Dublin 2, Ireland (a division of Penguin Books Ltd.).
Penguin Group (Australia), 250 Camberwell Road, Camberwell, Victoria 3124, Australia (a division of Pearson Australia Group Pty Ltd).
Penguin Books India Pvt Ltd, 11 Community Centre, Panchsheel Park, New Delhi - 110 017, India.
Penguin Group (NZ), Cnr Airborne and Rosedale Roads, Albany, Auckland 1310, New Zealand (a division of Pearson New Zealand Ltd).
Penguin Books (South Africa) (Pty) Ltd, 24 Sturdee Avenue, Rosebank, Johannesburg 2196, South Africa.
Penguin Books Ltd, Registered Offices: 80 Strand, London WC2R 0RL, England.

Published simultaneously in Canada. Manufactured in China by South China Printing Co. Ltd.
Design by Marikka Tamura. Text set in Cooper Old Style Demi. The art was done in soft pastels.
Library of Congress Cataloging-in-Publication Data
Kroll, Virginia L.   On the way to kindergarten / Virginia Kroll ; illustrated by Elisabeth Schlossberg.   p. cm.
Summary: A mother describes the increasing accomplishments of her five-year-old, from crying and sleeping, to riding a tricycle,
then preparing for school. [1. Babies—Fiction. 2. Children—Fiction. 3. Growth—Fiction. 4. Stories in rhyme.]
I. Schlossberg, Elisabeth, ill. II. Title.   PZ8.3.K8997On 2006   [E]—dc22   2004009263   ISBN 0-399-24168-X
1 3 5 7 9 10 8 6 4 2
First Impression